WHEN the SNOW is DEEPER THAN my BOOTS ARE TALL

GODWINBOOKS

Henry Holt and Company • New York

WHEN THE SNOW IS DEEPER THAN MY BOOTS ARE TALL

Jean Reidy   illustrations by **Joey Chou**

Jump up in the morning.
Winter's here at last!
Gobble down my pancakes.
Getting dressed so fast.

Find a frosty window.
Watch the flakes fall.
Look! The snow is deeper
than my toes are tall.

Slip on my snow pants.
Tug on my hat.
Loopty-loop my scarf.
What's cozier than that?
Zip up my jacket. Yes!
My, oh my!

Now the snow is deeper—
the snow is getting deeper—
the snow is deeper than my
ankles are high.

Step!

Stamp!

Tracks in the white.

Run!

Stomp!

Then I roll, roll, roll
that ball, ball, ball,
and the carrot-nosed man
grows tall, tall, tall.

Flakes on my tongue. Yum!

Pat a frozen pie.
Now the snow is deeper—
it's getting so much deeper—

the snow is deeper
than my shins are high.

But my pinkie's in my mitten
where my thumb should go,
and my hat flies off
when the cold winds blow,

and my nose drip, drips,
and my wet cheeks freeze,

and the drifts, oh they drift
to the tops of my knees,
and my feet get soaked,
toes one and all,
because the snow is deeper—
it's really so much deeper—

the snow is deeper than my boots are tall.

Papa to
my rescue.

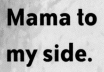

Mama to
my side.

Kissing on my
cheek where my
smile tries to hide.

Loving arms around me,
swooped up in the sky.

Because my papa's taller—
my mama's taller—
we're all tall-taller
than the snow is high.

Then we drop, plop, flop
in a frosty feather bed,
and we laze as we gaze
at the blue overhead,

and we sweep our angel wings
through that bright white rug,
because the snow is softer
than a winter's day hug.

Stardust from the heavens
far as I can see,

because it's **"OH!"**
much bigger,

it's **"WHOA!"**
much bigger,

it's **SO much bigger**
than you and me.

Heading in the house
where the burning
logs snap.

Off with my wet socks.
Off with my cap.

Stirring up the cocoa
in my cozy blue mug.
Then I snuggle right in
like a little beetle bug.

Let the flakes out my window
just fall, fall, fall.

When my heart's so big . . .

I never feel small.

To Erin —J. R.

**To Mom and Dad,
and our first snow together
in Mount Hehuan** —J. C.

Henry Holt and Company, *Publishers since 1866*
Henry Holt® is a registered trademark of Macmillan Publishing Group, LLC
120 Broadway, New York, NY 10271 • mackids.com

Text copyright © 2019 by Jean Reidy
Illustrations copyright © 2019 by Joey Chou
Library of Congress Control Number 2019932414
ISBN 978-1-250-12712-9

Our books may be purchased in bulk for promotional, educational, or business use. Please contact your local
bookseller or the Macmillan Corporate and Premium Sales Department at (800) 221-7945 ext. 5442
or by email at MacmillanSpecialMarkets@macmillan.com.

First edition, 2019 / Designed by Liz Dresner
The illustrations in this book were digitally painted in Adobe Photoshop.
Printed in China by Hung Hing Off-set Printing Co. Ltd., Heshan City, Guangdong Province

1 3 5 7 9 10 8 6 4 2